Simon & Schuster Books for Young Readers

An imprint of Simon & Schuster Children's Publishing Division

1230 Avenue of the Americas, New York, New York 10020

Text copyright © 2001 by Melinda Long

Illustrations copyright © 2001 by Thor Wickstrom

Book design by Heather Wood

The text for this book is set in Fairfield Medium.

The illustrations are rendered in oil and paper.

Printed in Hong Kong

First Edition

10   9   8   7   6   5   4   3   2   1

Library of Congress Cataloging-in-Publication Data

Long, Melinda.

Hiccup snickup / by Melinda Long ; illustrated by Thor Wickstrom.

p. cm.

Summary : Acting on the advice of various family members, a child tries different ways to get rid of the hiccups.

ISBN 0-689-82245-6

[1. Hiccups—Fiction.] I. Wickstrom, Thor, ill. II. Title.

PZ7.L856 Hi 2001   [E]—dc21   99-462277

To *my mother*,

    who taught me to love reading,

my father,

    who taught me to love stories,

and to Grandma Huskey,

    who taught me how to cure the hiccups

           —**M. L.**

To *all the kids*

    at the Robert C. Parker School

           —**T. W.**

Today, between breakfast and snacktime, a terrible thing happened. It was a thing worse than eating spinach . . . worse than listening to my brother practice his tuba . . . worse, even, than having to kiss my great-aunt Hattie.

I got the hiccups.

Every time I opened my mouth
to talk, a big **HIC** came out.
I couldn't even eat my peanut
butter crackers for hiccuping.

I was miserable.

I asked Grandma what I should do.
Right away she said:

Hiccup snickup
Rear right straight up.
Three drops in the teacup
Will cure the hiccups.

"Three drops *HIC* of what?" I asked her.

Hic!

"Don't ask me!" said Grandma. "It's just something my mother always used to say."

She told me to say it three times fast, and the hiccups would go away.

I decided to try.

Hiccup snickup
Rear right straight up.
Three drops in the teacup
Will cure the hiccups.

I walked straight into Mama. "I see you've been talking to Grandma," she said. "Did she tell you to say it three times fast?"

"I can barely say it one time *HIC* slowly," I told her.

She rubbed my head and handed me a big paper bag with holes cut out for eyes, and an apple. "Have you tried the paper bag trick?" she asked.

hic?

So there I was, walking down the hall with a paper bag over my head, eating an apple, and saying,

"Hiccups?" It was my sister, Jenny. She knows everything.

"*HIC.*" I nodded.

"Try drinking water from the wrong side of a cup," she suggested.

hic!

I did.
I got wet.
The hiccups didn't go away.

hic!

So there I was with a wet shirt, a bag over my head, eating an apple, and saying,

crunch, munch.

Hic!

Hiccup snickup
Rear right straight up.
Three drops in the teacup
Will cure the hiccups.

. . . when I almost tripped over my little brother, Sam.

"BOO!" he yelled.

I fell backward onto the kitchen floor.
"What'd you *HIC* do that for?" I asked him.

He shrugged. "I guess scaring
doesn't work after all," he said,
and then walked off to raid the
refrigerator.

So there I was, scared to death, with a wet shirt, a bag over my head, eating an apple, and saying,

Hiccup snickup (brrr!)
Rear right straight up.(hic.)
Three drops in the teacup (crunch.)
Will cure the hiccups.(hic!)

My older brother, Joey, who wants to be a doctor, sat down beside me. "Hold your breath," he ordered, "and stand on your cranium."

So there I was, scared to death, in a wet shirt, wearing a paper bag and eating an apple, while standing on my head, holding my breath, and saying,

Hiccup snickup
Rear right straight up.
Three drops in the teacup
Will cure the hiccups.

That's when my dad came along. "Are you okay?" he asked.

"*HIC*," I answered.

Hic!

Dad helped me up and pulled the bag off my head.

"Now what was it you were saying?"

I told him about "Hiccup snickup."

"Oh! I remember that one!" he said. "But you're missing something important."

"I *HIC* am?"

"Yes," he answered.
"Close your eyes."

"Take a deep breath," Mom added,
coming into the kitchen.

"Turn your head sideways," Joey told me.

"Stick your finger in your ear," said Sam between bites of an apple.

"Hold your tongue," Jenny piped in, poking her head around the corner.

"Nonsense!" Grandma called from the hallway. Everybody turned to listen. Everybody always listens when Grandma speaks. "All you need is a little help." said Grandma.

"From all of us," Grandma answered. "Just like this."
She started out fast and got faster.

We were laughing so hard by the time we were finished that I hardly noticed I wasn't hiccuping anymore.

"I guess three drops in the teacup really do cure the hiccups," I told them.

Nobody answered.
They couldn't.

The only thing they could say was, "Hic!"